TEDDY BEAR POSTMAN

by Phoebe and Selby Worthington

FREDERICK WARNE

For John

Copyright © 1981 Frederick Warne (Publishers) Ltd
First published 1981 by Frederick Warne (Publishers) Ltd, London
Reprinted 1983

ISBN 0 7232 2768 3

Phototypeset by Tradespools Ltd, Frome, Somerset
Printed by Clark Constable (1982) Ltd, Edinburgh
D7177.1083

Once upon a time there was a Teddy Bear Postman who lived all by himself. He had a cap with a
badge, and a bag for the letters and cards.

He got up very early every morning, except on Sundays. Sometimes, in the winter, it was still dark.

One Christmas Eve the Teddy Bear Postman
went to the station to pick up the sacks of mail.

He pushed the sacks on a handcart to the Post
Office. BUMPETY-BUMPETY-BUMP, BUMPETY-
BUMPETY-BUMP.

The Teddy Bear Postman sat on a high stool and stamped the letters and parcels. BANG! BANG! BANG! he went. BANG! BANG! BANG! The Post Mistress brought him a nice hot drink.

He found a parcel that had not been packed properly. A pretty doll was slipping out of it, so he got some more paper and string, and wrapped her up carefully.

He took the parcels and the letters and the cards
to the right houses. Everyone was pleased to see
him.

When he came to the doll's new home the little dog who lived there ran to meet him.

The lady said, 'Merry Christmas, Mr Postman!
Come in and have a mince pie and a glass of
ginger wine.'

When he had visited all the houses, the Teddy
Bear Postman opened the pillar-box in the street
and emptied all the letters into his bag. He took
them back to the Post Office to be sorted.

He was very tired when he got home so he had a hot bath.

The Teddy Bear Postman ate his supper in front of the fire and wondered what was in his own parcels.

Then he went upstairs, hung up his stocking and climbed into bed. Very soon he was fast asleep.

And that is the story of the Teddy Bear Postman.